*For Hugh*
–J.C.

**tiger tales**

an imprint of ME Media, LLC

202 Old Ridgefield Road, Wilton, CT 06897

Published in the United States 2007

Originally published in Great Britain 2006

by Little Tiger Press

an imprint of Magi Publications

Text copyright ©2006 Christine Leeson

Illustrations copyright ©2006 Jane Chapman

CIP Data is available

ISBN-13: 978-1-58925-068-0

ISBN-10: 1-58925-068-0

Printed in China

1 3 5 7 9 10 8 6 4 2

# The Snow Angel

by Christine Leeson     Illustrated by Jane Chapman

tiger tales

It was a bright, crisp morning when a swirl of wind woke Daisy.

"Mom! Sam! Wake up," she squeaked. "It's Christmas! And it's snowing!"

"Yippee!" cheered Daisy's big brother, Sam, dancing around the nest. "Merry Christmas, everyone!"

"Merry Christmas, little ones," said Mom, giving them each a gift.

"Oooh!" Daisy squealed. "Berries!"

"And nuts!" said Sam. "Thanks, Mom!"

Saving their presents
for later, the mice rushed
out to play in the snow.
"Have fun!" Mom
called. "I'll find some
extra bedding to make
our nest cozy, and then
we'll have a special
Christmas dinner."

Giggling, Daisy and Sam slipped and slid up the hill. Below sparkled a blanket of snow, but Daisy and Sam hardly noticed. High above was the most beautiful thing they'd ever seen. Sunshine gleamed on its wings as it soared through the sky.

"Sam, look," whispered Daisy. "It's an angel! A Christmas angel!"

But as the mice watched breathlessly, the angel began to flutter and fall.

"Oh no!" cried Daisy, rushing forward as it tumbled to the ground.

"Quick!" Sam gasped.

With whiskers trembling,
the mice tiptoed over the snow.

The angel was lying silent and still. Its feathers
shone like ice, and snow crystals glittered on its wings.
"Oh, Sam!" Daisy cried. "Isn't it wonderful?"
"I don't think it looks very well," Sam replied.

Then the snowy angel spoke. "Little mice, can you help me?" it said. "My friends and I have flown for days from a land of ice and stars, but last night I lost them in a storm. Now I'm tired and hungry, and I don't know if I will ever see them again."

"Oh, dear! We need to find food," said Daisy, "but everything is frozen."

"Not everything,"
said Sam. "Come on!"
And the mice raced
off across the meadow.

The snow was much deeper when the mice returned, carrying their precious gifts of berries and nuts. They placed them in front of the angel and watched as, slowly, it began to eat.

Daisy brushed snowflakes from the angel's
wings as it lay its head down to sleep.
"Do you think it will be all right?" she asked.
"I hope so," said Sam.

They waited by the angel's side
until at last the snow stopped falling
and sunset streaked the sky. Then
the angel opened its eyes.

With a sudden rush of
feathers, it spread its wings.
    "Thank you, little mice,"
it said. "You have been very
kind. I will never forget your help."

The mice gasped as the angel,
shining gold in the evening light,
soared up over their heads.
"Merry Christmas!" it called.
"Wow!" whispered Sam.

Daisy held up her paws.
"Look!" she cried. "It's
snowing again!"
White flakes whirled
around them, but as Sam
reached out and caught
one, he laughed in surprise.
"Feathers!" he shouted.

The mice gathered
armfuls of soft, white
feathers and raced
back home.

"Mom!" called Daisy.
"We found an angel!
It gave us a present!"

Mom looked up from the straw she'd been using to line their nest.

"Goose feathers!" she exclaimed. "We'll feel as if we're sleeping on clouds!"

Over Christmas dinner, Daisy and
Sam told Mom all about their snow
angel. Then, happy and tired, the family
snuggled up on a warm bed of feathers.

"This was the best Christmas ever!"
Daisy whispered to Sam. "We did see
a real angel, didn't we?"

"I'm sure we did," said Sam.

And, as he drifted off to sleep, he saw
the feathers shining in the darkness,
twinkling like stars in a frosty winter sky.

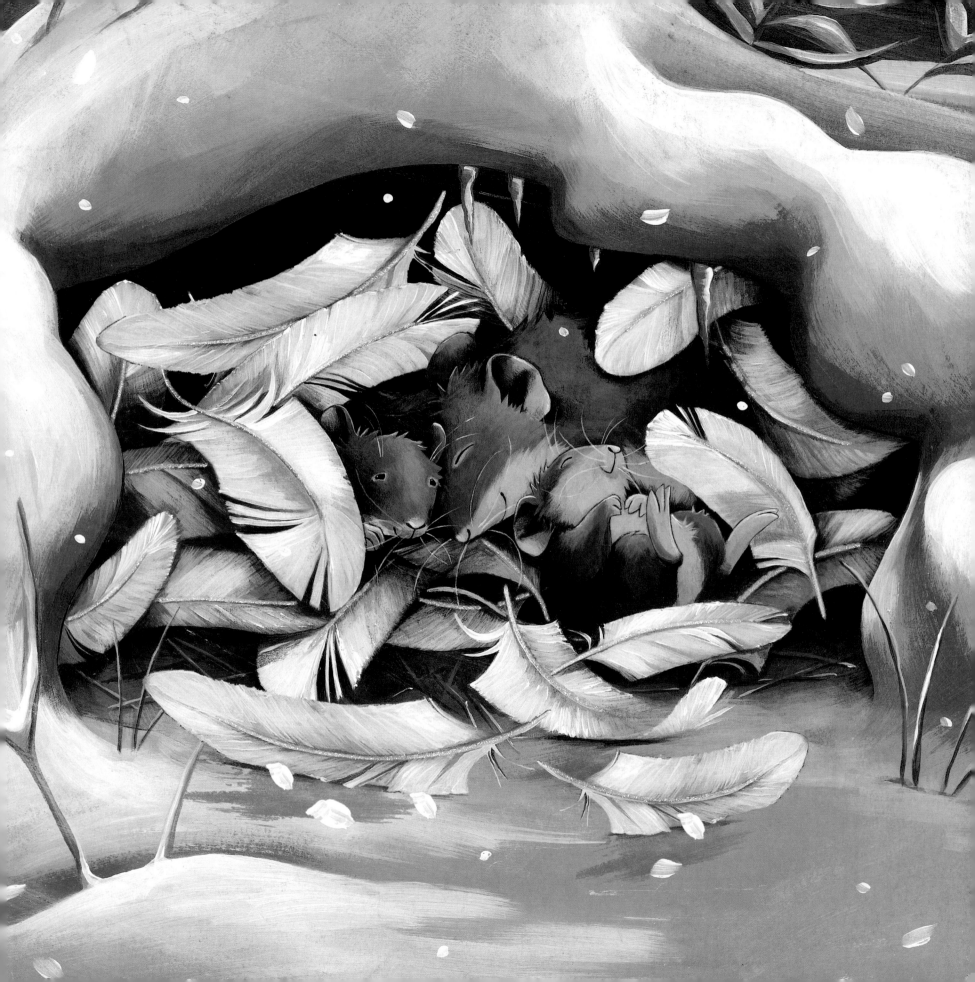